BOTSWANA

...in Pictures

Visual Geography Series®

BOTSWANA

...in Pictures

Prepared by
Thomas O'Toole

Lerner Publications Company
Minneapolis

VISUAL GEOGRAPHY SERIES®

Publisher
Harry Jonas Lerner
Associate Publisher
Nancy M. Campbell
Senior Editor
Mary M. Rodgers
Editors
Gretchen Bratvold
Dan Filbin
Phyllis Schuster
Photo Researchers
Karen A. Sirvaitis
Kerstin Coyle
Editorial/Photo Assistant
Marybeth Campbell
Consultants/Contributors
Thomas O'Toole
Sandra K. Davis
Designer
Jim Simondet
Cartographer
Carol F. Barrett
Indexers
Kristine S. Schubert
Sylvia Timian
Production Manager
Gary J. Hansen

Courtesy of Charlie Hurd

**Dust flies as Botswanan workers blast through rock to build
a new road.**

This book is a newly commissioned title in the Visual
Geography Series. The text is set in 10/12 Century
Textbook.

LIBRARY OF CONGRESS CATALOGING-IN-PUBLICATION DATA

O'Toole, Thomas, 1941–

  Botswana in pictures / prepared by Thomas O'Toole.
    p.   cm. − (Visual geography series)
  Includes index.
  Summary: An introduction to the geography, history,
government, economy, culture, and people of Botswana,
a landlocked country in southern Africa.
  ISBN 0-8225-1856-2
  1. Botswana. [1. Botswana.] I. Title. II. Series:
Visual geography series (Minneapolis, Minn.)
DT791.086   1990
968.83—dc20   89-13103
                                        CIP
                                         AC

International Standard Book Number: 0-8225-1856-2
Library of Congress Catalog Card Number: 89-13103

Courtesy of Department of Information and Broadcasting

Four ostriches cross the grasslands of Botswana.

Acknowledgments

Title page photo by Michael Kahn/The Hutchison
Library.

Elevation contours adapted from *The Times Atlas of
the World,* seventh comprehensive edition (New York:
Times Books, 1985).

1 2 3 4 5 6 7 8 9 10 99 98 97 96 95 94 93 92 91 90

The Kalahari Desert covers 100,000 square miles of Botswana, South Africa, and Namibia. Within Botswana, characteristic sand dunes exist only in the southwestern portions of the desert.

Contents

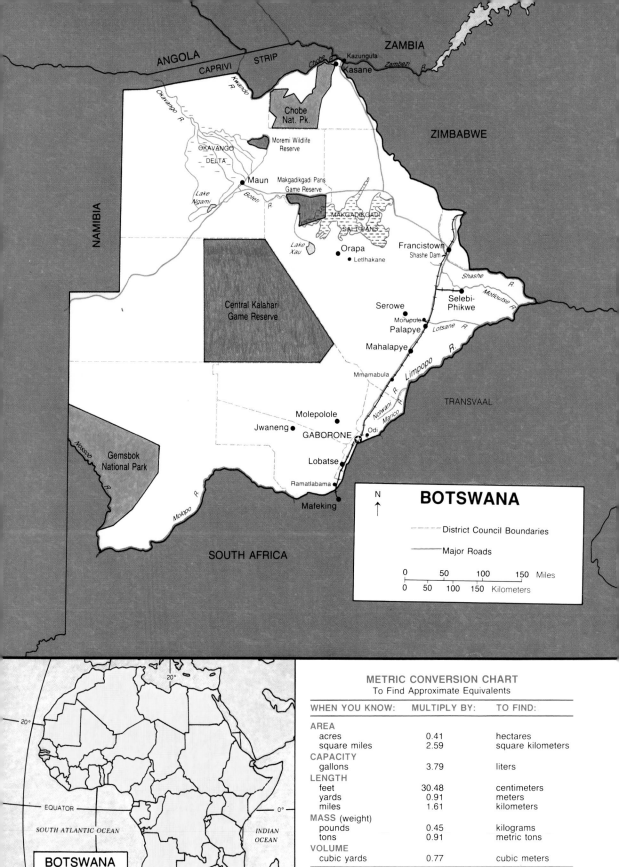

ANGOLA
CAPRIVI STRIP
ZAMBIA
Kazungula
Kasane
Zambezi R.
Chobe R.

Chobe
Nat. Pk.

ZIMBABWE

Kwando R.
Okavango R.
OKAVANGO DELTA

Moremi Wildlife
Reserve

NAMIBIA

Lake
Ngami
Maun
Boteti R.

Makgadikgadi Pans
Game Reserve

MAKGADIKGADI
SALT PANS

Lake
Xau
Orapa
Letlhakane
Francistown
Shashe Dam
Shashe R.
Motloutse R.

Central Kalahari
Game Reserve

Serowe
Selebi-
Phikwe
Morupule
Palapye
Lotsane R.
Mahalapye

Mmamabula
Limpopo R.

TRANSVAAL

Molepolole
Jwaneng
GABORONE
Notwani R.
Marico R.
Odi

Nossob R.
Gemsbok
National Park

Lobatse

Ramatlabama
Molopo R.
Mafeking

SOUTH AFRICA

N

BOTSWANA

‒ ‒ ‒ District Council Boundaries

⎯⎯⎯ Major Roads

| 0 | 50 | 100 | 150 | Miles |
| 0 | 50 | 100 | 150 | Kilometers |

20°
20°
EQUATOR 0°
SOUTH ATLANTIC OCEAN
INDIAN OCEAN
20°

BOTSWANA
AFRICA

| 0 | 1000 Miles |
| 0 | 1000 Kilometers |

20° 0° 40°

METRIC CONVERSION CHART
To Find Approximate Equivalents

WHEN YOU KNOW:	MULTIPLY BY:	TO FIND:
AREA		
acres	0.41	hectares
square miles	2.59	square kilometers
CAPACITY		
gallons	3.79	liters
LENGTH		
feet	30.48	centimeters
yards	0.91	meters
miles	1.61	kilometers
MASS (weight)		
pounds	0.45	kilograms
tons	0.91	metric tons
VOLUME		
cubic yards	0.77	cubic meters
TEMPERATURE		
degrees Fahrenheit	0.56 (*after* subtracting 32)	degrees Celsius

The town plan of Mahalapye is made up of numerous family units, each of which is encircled by a hedge. Shade trees, under which cooking and eating take place, are usually included in the compound.

Introduction

A landlocked country in southern Africa, Botswana is mostly semidesert and scrubland. Inhabited for centuries by a nomadic people called the San, the nation is now dominated by the Batswana, after whom the country is named. (The Batswana are distinct from Botswanans, which refers to all of the nation's citizens.)

Ancestors of the earliest Batswana began moving into the region from central Africa about 2,000 years ago. In time, they formed eight major kingdoms, each occupying its own territory. But the Batswana were unable to avoid Great Britain when it took an interest in the area. By 1895 Britain had claimed the lands of the Ba-

tswana as part of its colonial African empire. In 1966 Botswana achieved independence from British authority.

Since gaining self-rule, Botswana has had two presidents. Seretse Khama headed the government from 1966 until his death in 1980. Quett Masire, the vice president, succeeded Seretse Khama as president and was elected to the office in his own right in 1984.

Although increasingly a unified nation, Botswana contains several ethnic and language groups. Most Botswanans are Batswana cattle herders and farmers who speak a Bantu language called Setswana. In the west and south dwell the San, who

7

use a distinctive language characterized by its clicking sounds. Long-established patterns of livestock ownership enable a small group of wealthy Batswana to own most of the cattle and land.

Few Botswanans can live solely on their farming income. As a result, many people seek jobs in South Africa—Botswana's southern neighbor. In fact, Botswanans are a major source of labor for South Africa's mines. The modern foundation of Botswana's own economy is also mining.

With the aid of the national government, international corporations—some of which are based in South Africa—run Botswana's mining operations.

President Masire seeks ways to reduce the country's dependence on South Africa and to develop economic ties with other nations. His government also wants to enable more people to own land and cattle. If the nation achieves these goals, the coming decades may bring prosperity to a greater number of Botswanans.

Courtesy of Charlie Hurd

A merchant stands beside his display of goods in Lobatse—the center of Botswana's vital cattle-processing industry.

Surrounded by scrub vegetation, a baobab tree overlooks the Chobe River, which winds through northern Botswana.

Courtesy of Peter Lodoen

1) The Land

Botswana—a landlocked country with more than 231,000 square miles of territory —is about the size of the state of Texas. To the east is Zimbabwe, and South Africa lies to the east and south. Namibia borders Botswana to the west, and the Caprivi Strip—an extension of Namibia—stretches along Botswana's northern frontier. The nation also shares a short boundary with Zambia near the northern city of Kasane on the Zambezi River.

Topography

Most of Botswana consists of flat, elevated land with numerous low hills. The highest point in the country is Otse Mountain, which rises to 4,886 feet in southeastern

In northwestern Botswana, the Tsodilo Hills rise to heights of several thousand feet. Local people call the individual hills male, female, and child, depending on the size.

Botswana. Other uplands lie in the northwest, where the Tsodilo Hills are the tallest peaks. This region is noted for its multicolored stone and for hundreds of rock paintings dating from about 4,000 years ago.

The Kalahari Desert, part of a large plateau that covers southern Africa, dominates the southern two-thirds of the nation. Stretching into Namibia and South Africa, the Kalahari has an almost uniform altitude of about 3,300 feet above sea level. Only isolated pockets, such as the sand dunes of the southwestern corner, reflect true desert conditions. In these areas, little vegetation grows.

Much of the rest of the Kalahari is covered with seasonal grasses, and small

In the wet season, water lilies cluster on the Okavango Delta—a swampy area in the northwestern part of Botswana through which the Okavango River flows.

sections consist of rocky plains with occasional thorny shrubs. Although ancient waterways have dried up, underground water is close enough to the surface to support some plant life. Rivers, such as the Molopo and the Nossob, appear in the desert in the wet season.

Northwestern Botswana is made up of a vast inland delta (a swampy area) created by the Okavango River and its branches. As the river flows southeastward from Angola, it carries about two million tons of sand and silt into the swampland each year.

Covering more than 4,000 square miles, the broad delta has strong agricultural potential because it has rich soil. At present, however, the region is too wet to farm. Some of the Okavango's water volume goes to marshy Lake Ngami. Outflow from the Okavango also reaches the Boteti River and eventually enters Lake Xau and the

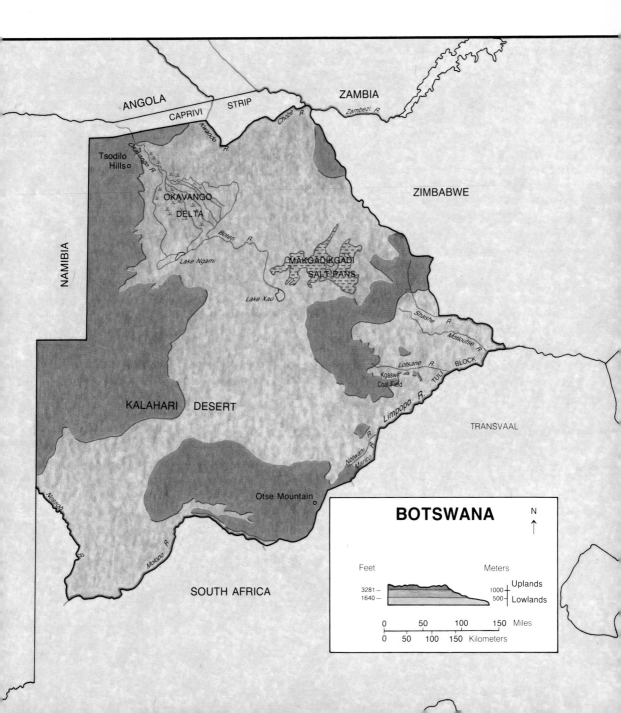

Makgadikgadi Salt Pans located in northeastern Botswana.

The Makgadikgadi Salt Pans are shallow depressions where small amounts of brackish (salty) water collect when the rains come. Thousands of years ago, these pans were the site of a large lake. A change in climate caused the lake to evaporate, leaving behind a salty deposit. Fed by the Okavango and Boteti rivers, the region changes from wetland to semi-arid country with the seasons. In the dry period, water in the pans is sometimes only a few inches deep.

Rivers and Lakes

Water—and its absence—deeply influences the lives of people and animals in Botswana. Indeed, the name of the country's unit of money—the pula—means "rain" in Setswana (the national language), and "let there be rain" is a formal greeting between Botswanans. Except for the Okavango river system, none of Botswana's waterways flows throughout the year. Rivers carry surface water during the rainy season, and in the Kalahari Desert water collects in shallow lakes that form immediately after a rainfall.

Courtesy of John C. Mason

After a recent rain, a freshly filled pan—or shallow depression—attracts birds and other wildlife to its banks.

Rising in Angola, the Okavango River travels southeastward for about 1,000 miles, forming a section of the Angola-Namibia border. The waterway then crosses the Caprivi Strip into Botswana. As it enters the nation's territory, the Okavango branches into a network of streams. The water from the river remains in Botswana and empties into the Okavango Delta.

The Limpopo River, which is about 1,000 miles long, separates the South African province of Transvaal from Botswana and Zimbabwe. Eventually, this waterway cuts through Mozambique and then flows into the Indian Ocean. Many Botswanans live near the fertile banks of the Limpopo and its tributaries.

In northern Botswana runs the Chobe River—a swampy, lower section of the longer Kwando River that travels through Angola and Zambia into the Zambezi

Courtesy of Claudia A. Hart

Elephants head for the cool waters of the Chobe River. These animals are becoming more rare in Africa as poachers kill them for their valuable ivory tusks. Botswana allows a limited amount of ivory trading.

A woman stands at the door of her house as a seasonal downpour drenches her compound. Droughts occurred throughout Botswana during the 1980s, but rains in 1988 arrived at normal levels.

River. The Chobe flows through Chobe National Park—a protected wildlife area. Short rivers—including the Motloutse, Lotsane, Marico, and Notwani—drain the eastern hilly section of the country. This seasonally watered region contains all of the nation's major cities. Boreholes (deeply drilled wells) reach underground water, which serves the needs of these urban areas.

Botswana has few lakes. The first European to see Lake Ngami, in the northwest, was the British missionary and explorer David Livingstone, who found it in 1849. At that time, the lake covered about 90 square miles. Since then, it has shrunk and is sometimes very shallow. Lake Xau, a salty body of water, lies near the center of Botswana, just south of the Makgadikgadi Salt Pans.

Climate

Because Botswana is situated in the Southern Hemisphere, winter occurs between May and September, and summer comes between October and April. The nation's location in the subtropical belt of the African continent makes average daytime temperatures high.

Rain falls unevenly in Botswana and varies widely in amounts. In the north, annual precipitation averages from 17 to 25 inches. From east to west, rainfall decreases from about 21 inches in the northeast to about 13 inches in the northwest. The Kalahari Desert receives about 9 inches of rain—often much less—each year. The entire country is subject to periodic droughts, such as the ones that occurred in the 1960s and the 1980s. Hot, dry winds carry sand from the Kalahari Desert across the country in August.

Botswana lies at an average altitude of approximately 3,300 feet. Because of the elevation, the climate is hot during the day and quite cool at night. The warmest places in Botswana are in the north at Kasane and Maun. Between October and April, the hottest part of the year, temperatures can rise

13

The colorful orange blossoms of a flame tree—so named because its flowers make the plant appear to be on fire—brighten Botswana's landscape.

At the Moremi Wildlife Reserve, a small group of impalas (antelope) makes its way through the vegetation. Impalas prefer to live on the outskirts of forests, eating the low shrubbery. When frightened, the herd scatters, and these slight animals can leap as high as 30 feet in the air to escape predators.

to 100° F in the middle of the day. In the coldest months (June and July), temperatures often fall below 32° F at night, and frosts frequently occur.

Flora and Fauna

The natural distribution of Botswana's vegetation is closely related to rainfall. The drier parts of the Kalahari feature shrub grasslands, and the wetter sections contain trees. The moist northeast produces tree savanna (a mixture of trees and grass), and small areas of Botswana are forested. Acacias are the most common tree species in the country. True forests occur only on the banks of the Chobe River. Bloodwood, baobab, and teak trees grow in other areas.

The Okavango Delta abounds with birds and mammals, including elephants, zebras, buffalo, wildebeests, giraffes, hippopotamuses, and kudu (antelope with spirally twisted horns). Other kinds of antelope— as well as lions, leopards, and crocodiles—

also live in the country. Poisonous snakes, such as cobras and puff adders, are quite common, as are many varieties of scorpions, spiders, and termites. Ostriches, pelicans, flamingos, and bustards are among the many bird species that reside in Botswana. The principal fish, found mostly in the Chobe and Okavango rivers, include tilapia, tiger fish, and catfish.

The government of Botswana has set aside thousands of square miles of national territory as wildlife sanctuaries. Among the largest national parks in Botswana are Chobe in the north and Gemsbok in the southwest. Laws also protect animals on reserves, such as the Central Kalahari Game Reserve, the Makgadikgadi Pans Game Reserve, and the Moremi Wildlife Reserve in the Okavango Delta. In addition, the government carefully monitors about 40 hunting blocks, where hunters may shoot small quantities of game. Authorities issue only a limited number of shooting permits each year.

Natural Resources

Although many of Botswana's natural resources are underdeveloped, geologists have identified deposits of several valuable

Courtesy of Department of Information and Broadcasting

Botswana's zebra population is fairly large, and herds of dozens or more may graze on short grasses. The distinctive pattern on the hides of these horselike animals allows zebras to blend in with the surroundings and thereby to evade enemies.

Courtesy of Department of Information and Broadcasting

Discovered in 1976, the diamond deposits at Jwaneng in southeastern Botswana began yielding gems in 1982.

materials. Nickel and copper exist in the northeast near the city of Selebi-Phikwe. Supplies of coal, gold, silver, natural gas, and manganese have also been found in small quantities.

Gem-quality diamonds, which have been mined since the 1970s, lie in Orapa, Letlhakane, and Jwaneng. Botswana earns substantial export income from its diamond industry, which the government and a South African company jointly run.

Cities and Towns

Most Botswanans live in the eastern third of the country. More than 80 percent of the population inhabit rural areas, although cities and towns are expanding rapidly. The number of urban residents increases by more than 10 percent each year, compared to an annual growth rate of about 4 percent for rural sections. Much of the increase in the number of city dwellers occurs because villagers move to urban areas in search of jobs.

Courtesy of John C. Mason

In Serowe – a town in east central Botswana – the residents arrange their houses in a traditional pattern. Called *rondavels*, the homes are made of mud and have straw roofs.

Gaborone — the modern capital of Botswana — has steadily grown since independence in 1966. This archway leads to a new mall in the city.

Located in southeastern Botswana, the capital city of Gaborone has become a major administrative center since the country gained independence. Its 95,000 residents live in a carefully planned city, with modern buildings and neighborhoods. A broad street called the Mall cuts through the middle of the capital, and legislative and municipal structures lie at both ends of this main thoroughfare. The government of Botswana is Gaborone's chief employer.

A large population of white people, many of South African origin, dominates Francistown (population 34,000). Lying in northeastern Botswana near the Zimbabwean border, the city has developed from a minor gold-rush town into a commercial center. Recent finds of precious minerals have increased the importance of Francistown, which also serves as the starting point for many tourist journeys into the nation's wildlife parks.

From the air, Gaborone's gridlike street design and new buildings suggest its expansion from a small settlement — which the British colonial administration called Gaberones — into Botswana's largest population center.

17

Selebi-Phikwe, the third largest city in the country, has grown from a small agricultural village into a mining community of about 33,000. Located in northeastern Botswana, Selebi-Phikwe is linked to Gaborone by railways and roads. Comfortable residential areas surround Selebi-Phikwe. Mines, an ore-processing plant, an electrical factory, and other industrial sites are on the outskirts. Squatter settlements—where unemployed mine workers stay in the hope of finding jobs—have grown near the city.

Lying about 100 miles southwest of Selebi-Phikwe, Serowe (population 25,000)

is the chief city of the Bangwato. This Batswana group once controlled the largest kingdom in the country. In the 1990s, Serowe still follows the layout of a traditional village, with many round dwellings and a central meeting place.

Lobatse (population 20,000) in southeastern Botswana is the hub of the nation's cattle-processing industry. The city's slaughterhouse is one of the largest plants of its kind in Africa. Most local businesses involve or support the livestock trade, although craft industries also exist. In addition, Lobatse serves as the site of Botswana's highest court.

Potential customers browse among the shops in Selebi-Phikwe—a town that has developed with Botswana's copper-mining industry.

18

Archaeologists are not certain who painted the rock illustrations in the Tsodilo Hills of northwestern Botswana. The region contains many depictions of animals, along with some geometric patterns and handprints.

2) History and Government

Archaeologists have found evidence of early settlement and migration in Botswana. These findings suggest that the nation has had an important role in southern African history.

As long as two million years ago, ancestors of early humans lived in Botswana. By about 50,000 years ago, the region's inhabitants looked very much like modern human beings. The early residents of Botswana used stone tools, hunted game, and gathered plants. Cave paintings found in the area depict some of the animals, including antelope and hippos, that lived among the hunting and gathering peoples.

Early Inhabitants

From these original communities developed the San and the Khoikhoi, whose descendants still dwell in Botswana. (Europeans later named the San "Bushmen" and

19

called the Khoikhoi "Hottentots.") About 3,000 years ago, these two African groups were well established throughout southern Africa. They had uncomplicated social and political structures, and various bands competed for the area's water and food.

The San were skilled hunters, using light bows and poison-tipped arrows to kill their prey. San women gathered plants, and San men provided meat and fish. The Khoikhoi hunted and gathered, but—unlike the San—they also kept livestock, primarily sheep and cattle. Evidence suggests that in Botswana the San lived mostly in the southwest and northwest and that the Khoikhoi occupied the center and north of the country. Cave paintings found in the Tsodilo Hills date from about 4,000 years ago and illustrate the daily lives of these early peoples.

Perhaps as a result of the Khoikhoi's ownership of livestock, the ways of the San and Khoikhoi began to differ markedly. The San continued to hunt, gather, and live a nomadic life in small groupings. The Khoikhoi became herders of cattle and formed permanent villages.

BANTU MIGRATION

After centuries of competition for game, the San and the Khoikhoi encountered other ethnic groups. Sometime before A.D. 100, Bantu-speaking peoples began a gradual, southward migration from central Africa. These newcomers grew crops and used iron tools. Eventually, some of the Bantu-speakers intermarried with the San and the Khoikhoi and set up small agricultural villages. In Botswana, archaeological evidence suggests that farming communities existed near the site of Francistown, along the Chobe River, and in the Tsodilo Hills.

The arrival of the Bantu groups changed the way of life in Botswana. The newcomers brought tools and farming methods that allowed the area to support a greater number of people. Populations grew and village life became more structured.

As a result of the Bantu migration, knowledge of iron and smelting (an ore-melting process) became widespread. Between A.D. 1000 and 1250, mining sites rose in number. In addition, cattle herds and crop yields increased, helping the local populations to improve their food supply. The people in what is now Botswana eventually exchanged products with related ethnic groups in other parts of southern Africa. Commercial contacts developed in which copper, iron, gold, and ivory were the main trade items.

Independent Picture Service

Among Botswana's earliest inhabitants were the San—a people who lived by hunting and gathering their food. They used light bows and poison-tipped arrows to stun their carefully chosen prey. After felling the animal with poison, the hunter would spear it in the final step. This modern-day San hunter still follows the age-old lifestyle in the Kalahari Desert.

Baobab trees surround a site in northern Botswana that dates from about A.D. 100, when iron first came into use in the country. Bantu peoples from central Africa had developed iron-mining methods and brought that knowledge with them when they migrated southward about 2,000 years ago. With this new ability to use iron, local inhabitants developed trading and mining centers in southern Africa.

Courtesy of Eleanore Woollard

Using overland routes, traders took goods from landlocked Botswana to sites that had access to the sea. These trading centers, particularly the stations in Zimbabwe, flourished because of the sale of metals and ivory from Botswana and elsewhere.

Batswana Subgroups Form

Trading profits and farming surpluses strengthened the early Bantu groups and allowed them to form small, loosely organized communities. These groupings extended over a wide area in southern Africa, and by the early fourteenth century the units had become more defined. In Botswana, most of the people were concentrated in the north and east near plentiful water sources. Others lived outside Botswana along the southern African coasts.

As the number of people multiplied, large populations became harder to shelter and feed. Consequently, extended families split off from one another, establishing independent subgroups that often retained ties through marriage. During certain periods, droughts also caused communities to break up into smaller units and to spread over larger areas in search of food and water. By about 1300, the majority of

the Bantu peoples in Botswana belonged to the Batswana. This group spoke Setswana, a member of the Bantu family of languages. The Batswana further split into eight major subgroups, or clans, including the Bangwato, the Barolong, the Bakwena, the Batawana, and the Bakgatla.

SOCIAL ORGANIZATION

Each of the Batswana groups supported a strong social structure, the head of which was the clan's *kgosi,* or king. His son or another male relative inherited the *bogosi* (kingship) from him. The kgosi was not an all-powerful ruler. An assembly of adult males—called the *kgotla*—helped the king to decide matters of common interest.

People related to the ruler came next in the social organization and formed the top class. Ranked in the middle were members of nonroyal families, who often were part of the hunting parties, or *letsholo.* At the bottom were non-Batswana peoples, including the San and the Khoikhoi, who made up a manual labor pool.

Economic activities among the Batswana kingdoms centered on providing necessities, such as food, clothing, and housing. Herding livestock, farming small plots, hunting animals, and gathering food were common pursuits. Agriculture was

21

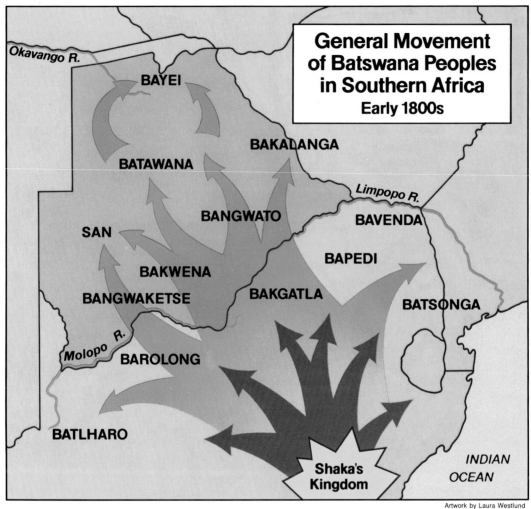

General Movement of Batswana Peoples in Southern Africa
Early 1800s

Okavango R.

BAYEI

BAKALANGA

BATAWANA

Limpopo R.

BANGWATO

BAVENDA

SAN

BAPEDI

BAKWENA

BANGWAKETSE

BAKGATLA

BATSONGA

Molopo R.

BAROLONG

BATLHARO

Shaka's Kingdom

INDIAN OCEAN

Artwork by Laura Westlund

The nation's dominant ethnic group is the Batswana, which includes eight major subgroups. Their ancestors arrived from other parts of Africa to escape droughts, overpopulation, and attacks by Shaka, the ruler of the Zulu realm. These movements occurred over several centuries. This map depicts the migrations of some of these peoples in the region. (Boundaries reflect current borders of Botswana and surrounding countries.) Map information from Thomas Tlou and Alec Campbell, *History of Botswana* (Gaborone: Macmillan Botswana, 1984).

not always successful because of the limited rainfall. Permanent settlements grew up near reliable supplies of water and provided a setting for political and social life.

In addition to owning large cattle herds, the king and the heads of stronger families collected tribute (payment) from weaker groups. Demanded mostly from non-Batswana peoples—such as the Bayei and Bakalanga—tribute paying caused considerable resentment between groups.

Emerging Conflicts

After 1600, more Batswana clans moved north and west from southern Africa into the open spaces of Botswana. Areas of settlement and trade contacts expanded with the arrival of these newcomers.

Meanwhile, in the early seventeenth century, Dutch merchants from the Netherlands established a foothold at the southern tip of the continent—a place called the Cape of Good Hope. By 1652 Dutch livestock farmers, known as Boers, had joined the Cape Colony. They claimed ownership of large expanses of African land, an activity that brought them in conflict with the Khoikhoi and the San.

Both African groups regarded the animals that the Dutch herded as wild and, therefore, as fair game for hunting. The Dutch disagreed and vowed to wipe out the African hunters. In the seventeenth and eighteenth centuries, the Dutch killed or enslaved most of the Khoikhoi. After decades of conflict that severely reduced their numbers, the San fled to the Kalahari Desert, where white settlers were unlikely to follow.

In time, the Boers also fought with many different Bantu-speaking groups about land usage and ownership. This warfare in what is now South Africa pushed more peoples toward Botswana. Thus, in the 1600s and 1700s, Botswana's population and area of settlement increased mainly through immigration.

The continuing pressure of Boer land claims in the south caused tensions among the Batswana, as well as among other Africans in the region. In former times, enough land had been available to satisfy the grazing and farming needs of all groups. Because of Boer activities, however, the Africans began to fight one another for limited pastureland. As a result of this warfare, one powerful ethnic group —the Zulu—came to dominate southern Africa.

In about 1815, a Zulu warrior-king named Shaka organized his followers into a skilled fighting force. The Zulu's warlike activities, which included taking over the lands of nearby African peoples, pushed many Batswana and related clans northward and westward. Some of the war refugees regrouped. Others completely left the area to escape the fighting, and many of these peoples ended up in Botswana. In the 1820s and 1830s, the *difaqane,* or forced migration caused by Zulu warfare, relocated many African groups.

Courtesy of Cape Archives Depot

Founder of the Zulu nation, Shaka emerged as the leader of a skilled fighting force in 1816. For the next 12 years, he and his troops took over the lands of the Batswana, chasing many clans into what is now Botswana. In 1828 Shaka's brothers judged him to be insane and killed him.

British Missionaries Arrive

A new foreign group—Christian missionaries—also began to make their presence felt in the 1820s. Members of the London Missionary Society, a Protestant organization based in Great Britain, ventured into the lands of the Batswana. Robert Moffat was among the earliest religious teachers to visit the area, but his efforts to convert Batswana clans to Christianity were not very successful.

Moffat's son-in-law, David Livingstone, set up a missionary station among the Bakwena near present-day Molepolole. Because of Livingstone's work, the Bakwena kgosi Sechele I was baptized in 1848. Livingstone also contacted other Batswana

23

clans. The warm welcome they gave him stemmed more from a hope of getting European weapons than from an enthusiasm for Christianity. Besides their religious purpose, British missionaries also wanted to explore undocumented areas of the continent and to encourage Africans to trade with Britain.

By the mid-nineteenth century, the Batswana came into increasing contact with various European communities as a result of warfare, trade, and missionary work. The Batswana bought European rifles to fight the descendents of the Boers—African-born whites called Afrikaners. The missionaries introduced European farming techniques and tools, which allowed powerful Batswana families to increase their harvests. They then traded the surplus crops for more European products, especially guns.

Among Livingstone's early converts to Christianity was the Bakwena *kgosi* (king) Sechele I. The king holds a fly whisk—a traditional African symbol of authority.

A Scottish doctor and Christian missionary, David Livingstone came to southern Africa as a young man in 1841. Landing on the coast, he mapped and explored inland areas, arriving at Lake Ngami in northern Botswana in 1849. Livingstone's later expeditions took him farther north, through Zambia, Tanzania, and Malawi, where he died in 1873.

Colonial Rule Established

Treks—Afrikaner migrations deeper into the African interior—began to restrict African settlements, especially after the Great Trek of 1835. In that year, hundreds of Afrikaner families packed their belongings into wagons and moved northeast into Bantu lands that are now part of Transvaal, South Africa. By the 1860s, their first territorial claims had widened, and precious minerals—gold and diamonds, for example—had been discovered. These finds made the Transvaal even more valuable to the Afrikaners, as well as to British investors.

The two groups clashed over control of the gold and diamond deposits. These conflicts temporarily distracted the Afrikaners from warfare with the Africans. As a result, during the 1850s and 1860s, the Batswana regained some stability after

About 15 miles from the town of Palapye lie the ruins of a missionary church. After the structure was abandoned in 1902, builders removed the roof and put it on a new church that they were constructing at Serowe.

Besides Christian religious practices and building styles, European missionaries also introduced Western farming techniques. In some areas of Botswana, farmers continue to use nineteenth-century methods to till their fields.

Khama III, kgosi of the Bangwato, first requested British protection against southern African whites in the 1870s. Initially, the British refused to safeguard his realm, but later they told Khama and other Batswana leaders that protection was in force. Throughout the remainder of his reign, Khama attempted to limit British interference in Bangwato affairs. He also opposed the move to make his lands part of South Africa.

the decades of the difaqane. Scattered groups formed larger units, and these new kingdoms obtained more guns to protect their lands from Afrikaner expansion.

In the 1870s, the threat of open hostilities between the Afrikaners and the Batswana increased. The Europeans regarded all land north, east, and west of the Transvaal as Afrikaner property. The Batswana groups who lived in these regions opposed these European territorial claims. One African ruler—the Bangwato king Khama III—asked the British for protection against the Afrikaners, but the British refused his request.

Meanwhile, other European powers, particularly Germany, had become interested in colonizing southern Africa. In time, Britain saw German influence in Africa as a threat to British trade. In 1885 the British told the Batswana that their lands —which the Europeans had dubbed Bechuanaland—were under British protection.

The British made the region south of the Molopo River—called British Bechuanaland—a colonial territory. The area north of the river was under British protection and was named the Bechuanaland Protectorate. Although the British government controlled the protectorate, the British did not claim legal ownership of the land. The creation of the protectorate allowed the British to block the advance of the Germans, who had taken over South-West Africa (present-day Namibia) in 1884. British authority also prevented the Afrikaners from claiming more land.

The Bechuanaland Protectorate

In theory, the government of the Bechuanaland Protectorate was in the hands of Batswana royal families. In practice, however, the British interfered in the internal affairs of the Batswana groups and set up their own governmental structure. The major function of this mixed local-colonial administration was to collect enough taxes to make the protectorate self-supporting.

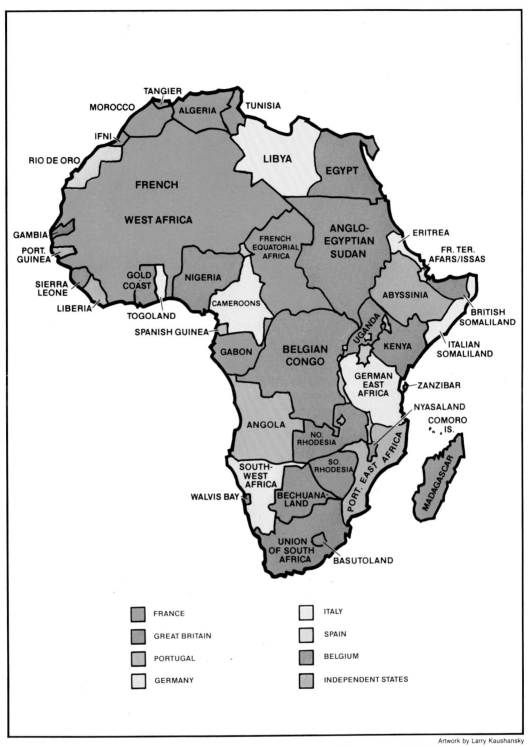

In the last decades of the 1800s, European powers scrambled to take control of vast tracts of the African continent. The British formed the Bechuanaland Protectorate from the territories of the Batswana in 1885. (Map information from *The Anchor Atlas of World History*, 1978.)

The Batswana kings protested when boundaries were drawn through traditional lands and often disagreed about where the new borders were placed. The kings were afraid that British laws might jeopardize the customary income from the payment of tribute.

Africans were also concerned about the activities of the British South Africa Company (BSAC)—a trading firm run by a wealthy politician named Cecil Rhodes. In the 1890s, Rhodes tried to gain control of Bechuanaland. He wanted to connect by rail his holdings in the Cape Colony (now Cape Province, South Africa) to his new lands in present-day Zimbabwe. To avoid

This small metal disk was a receipt given to an African for having paid a "hut tax" to the colonial authorities. The money raised by such payments helped officials to run the protectorate.

In a period cartoon, Cecil Rhodes, a South African politician, straddles the African continent from South Africa to Egypt. He believed this vast region should be linked by rail. Rhodes strongly encouraged the British to give him control of Bechuanaland to build the proposed railway. Rhodes planned the route of the track to run through his own lands in southern Africa.

Alarmed at Rhodes's campaign to control their kingdoms, three Batswana kings went to Britain. The efforts of Bathoen *(seated left),* Khama III *(seated right),* and Sebele *(standing left)* persuaded the British to reject the plan. Their interpreter and adviser was the missionary W. C. Willoughby *(standing right).*

conflicts with local leaders about land rights and to build the railroad quickly, Rhodes applied to the British for control of the protectorate. He argued that the railroad could foster a strong British presence in Africa by connecting the Cape Colony with lands far to the north.

In 1894 it seemed clear that the British would give Bechuanaland to Rhodes's company. The next year, Kings Khama (of the Bangwato), Bathoen (of the Bangwaketse), and Sebele (of the Bakwena) traveled to Great Britain to protest the proposed transfer. They gained the support of Christian groups and of British organizations that wanted to preserve African land rights. Because of the kings' efforts, the British government did not award Bechuanaland to Rhodes. Instead, the British gave the BSAC three narrow sections of land in eastern Bechuanaland on which to build a railway.

SOUTH AFRICAN PRESSURES

Great Britain safeguarded Bechuanaland from Rhodes, but the British assumed that the protectorate would eventually join the self-governing Union of South Africa. Afrikaner politicians established the union in 1910, and it absorbed British Bechuanaland that same year. Leaders of the independent Afrikaner state also wanted the Bechuanaland Protectorate to be under their control. But again the kings of several Batswana groups petitioned for Bechuanaland to remain under British authority. They saw harsh laws being passed in South Africa that limited or denied the rights of Africans. The kings did not want these same laws to govern them.

Although Afrikaner politicians petitioned British authorities many times to release the protectorate to them, the territory remained under British control. Nevertheless, the colonial administration

29

Gold and diamonds were discovered in South Africa in the mid-nineteenth century. By the early 1900s, the mining companies employed large numbers of Africans as low-paid laborers in the mines.

Independent Picture Service

did little to establish industries, roads, schools, or health services within the colony. In fact, the protectorate's British high commissioner maintained his headquarters in Mafeking, a city in South Africa.

The failure to develop trade, industries, and social services limited job opportunities in the colony. Many Africans in Bechuanaland were forced to work outside the protectorate, and some became migrant laborers in South Africa for very low wages. To some extent, the colonial government regarded Bechuanaland's population as a cheap labor pool and neglected the future of the colony.

Effects of World Wars I and II

Soon after the formation of the Union of South Africa in 1910, World War I (1914–1918) broke out. The conflict had little direct impact on the protectorate, whose soldiers fought with the British against Germany. As a result of postwar peace conferences, however, the German colony of South-West Africa came under the control of South Africa. Thereafter, white-ruled governments surrounded Bechuanaland.

Despite these international changes, the protectorate began to develop internally. In 1919 the British formed the Native Advisory Council (later called the African Council). The council advised the British high commissioner on African concerns.

At first, the council's representatives—the kings of major Batswana groups and their chosen associates—came only from the southern kingdoms. In 1931, however, the Batawana joined, and in 1940 the Bangwato sent their first delegates. Among the Bangwato representatives was

Tshekedi Khama, the guardian and uncle of the young, uncrowned kgosi, Seretse Khama, who was the grandson of Khama III.

At its meetings, the African Council expressed its continued opposition to union with South Africa. By the start of World War II (1939–1945), about half of the protectorate's African males between 15 and 44 were working in South Africa. The council's members worried about South Africa's increasingly harsh laws of apartheid (the Afrikaner word for apartness). These rules preserved and fostered the separateness of blacks and whites in South Africa and included restrictions on housing, landownership, and political rights for black South Africans.

During the war, the council supported Great Britain, and about 10,000 Batswana soldiers fought in the Middle East and Italy. Trained in the city of Lobatse, the troops formed anti-aircraft regiments and gun crews. Members of royal Batswana families participated in military expeditions to help Britain to achieve victory.

After the war, colonial authorities in Bechuanaland faced an entire generation of Africans who were neither herders, nor farmers, nor traditional leaders. These African manual laborers realized that apartheid could affect them very negatively. This view united African workers and the Batswana elite, who had long resisted becoming part of South Africa. As a result, both sections of Bechuanaland society began to support the idea of self-rule for the protectorate.

Seretse Khama and Independence

The royal marriage of the Bangwato kgosi, Seretse Khama, further stirred the fires of independence. In 1948, while studying in

Courtesy of R. L. Watson

A reserved bench in a South African waiting room is an example of apartheid—a policy of segregation that separates black people from white people. In the mid-twentieth century, South African laws increasingly restricted the rights of blacks. The Batswana kings, as well as the majority of Bechuanaland's African workers, strived to keep apartheid out of the protectorate.

Britain, Seretse Khama married a white Englishwoman named Ruth Williams. He returned to Bechuanaland in 1949 to take over the kingship. But his uncle Tshekedi Khama and other members of the traditional elite opposed his mixed marriage, as did the white-ruled governments of Southern Rhodesia (now Zimbabwe) and South Africa. To the colonial authorities, the tension seemed serious enough to justify keeping Tshekedi and Seretse apart. The British were also trying to please the pro-apartheid regimes in South Africa and Southern Rhodesia with whom Britain had strong economic ties.

In 1950, to calm the tense situation, the British government invited Seretse Khama to visit Great Britain. These same authorities then refused to allow him to return to Bechuanaland unless he gave up the kingship. The stated reason for this refusal was the rift between the nephew and his uncle, but the two men resolved their differences in 1952. Britain's continued restrictions on Seretse's freedom were based on its desire not to upset white-ruled South Africa.

For the next several years, many Bangwato in Bechuanaland protested Seretse's treatment by refusing to cooperate with the colonial government. But Seretse strongly desired to be of use to his country, and in 1956 he agreed not to accept the Bangwato kingship. Therefore, the British allowed him to return to Bechuanaland. After Seretse Khama's arrival in the protectorate in 1956, he immediately became vice chairperson of the Bangwato Council and a leader in the movement for self-rule.

POLITICAL PARTIES FORM

Also active at this time were the African politicians Philip G. Matante, Motsamai Mpho, and K. T. Motsete. In 1960 they formed the Bechuanaland Peoples' party (later Botswana Peoples' party, BPP). The BPP called for rapid social and political reform, a pro-African constitution, and the

Courtesy of Department of Information and Broadcasting

Born in 1921, Seretse Khama—heir to the kingship of the Bangwato—was educated in South Africa and Britain. His marriage in 1948 to a white Englishwoman sparked debates about racism and nationalism. After six years of forced exile, Seretse Khama returned to the protectorate in 1956 as a private citizen and became involved in the movement for self-rule. Shrewd as well as tolerant, Seretse eventually became the first president of the Republic of Botswana.

expulsion of white settlers. The party drew its followers from urban areas along the north-south railroad line in eastern Bechuanaland.

Choosing a more conservative program to achieve change, Seretse Khama and others formed the Bechuanaland (later Botswana) Democratic party (BDP). Although dominated by the Bangwato, Seretse Khama's party had widespread support.

Many Bangwato continued to follow Seretse Khama as their kgosi, and the traditional Batswana leaders accepted him as an equal. Some Africans who feared becoming part of South Africa identified with him because he had experienced Western prejudice. Europeans in Bechuanaland supported Seretse Khama and the BDP as the less harmful of two political choices. In fact, the British administration regarded him as the likely person to become the first prime minister of a self-ruling Bechuanaland.

In 1963 the British announced that a timetable for eventual independence had been set. Registration of African voters occurred in 1964, and the territory's first elections took place in 1965. Seretse Khama and the BDP—helped by the leader's power base and national reputation—won 80 percent of the votes and 28 out of 31 seats in the new legislative assembly. The BDP also received considerable financial support from liberal European settlers.

Seretse Khama became prime minister in 1965. He oversaw the peaceful transition of governmental authority from the Bechuanaland Protectorate to the Republic of Botswana. When the republic was established on September 30, 1966, Seretse Khama—who was knighted by Britain's Queen Elizabeth II in the same year—became its first president.

Courtesy of Eleanore Woollard

Improving Botswana's network of roads was among the major goals of the republic's early years.

The Republic's Early Years

Following independence, Seretse Khama pursued moderate policies, while facing the fact of Botswana's lack of development. The colonial government had not built a strong transportation network, had not established a good communications system, and had not started many industries. The new nation also lacked overland access to the sea except through white-ruled South Africa, South-West Africa (Namibia), and Southern Rhodesia (Zimbabwe). Botswana needed the manufactured goods, markets, and communication systems of these states to survive.

Despite this dependence, the new nation spoke out against the apartheid policies of South Africa and Southern Rhodesia. Botswana publicly supported black Africans' struggles for reform and liberation in these countries but continued to trade with them. In the meantime, the president improved relations with Great Britain and established links with other black-ruled nations in Africa. In these ways, Seretse Khama hoped to obtain funds for development projects within Botswana. He also wanted to reduce the domination of the Batswana ruling class, particularly regarding cattle ownership and land rights.

No matter how much the Botswana government tried, however, it could not remain completely aloof from tensions in neighboring states. Southern Rhodesia, for example, experienced a civil war between 1972 and 1979. Thousands of civilians and guerrilla fighters fled to Botswana for safety. On several occasions, Rhodesian bombers attacked refugee camps in Botswana. After Rhodesia became independent as Zimbabwe in 1980, the refugees returned to their homeland.

In the 1970s, Botswana also received exiles from white-ruled South Africa, and hostility sometimes erupted between the two countries. The South African government accused Botswana of protecting revolutionary groups—such as the outlawed African National Congress—that seek to

A statue of Seretse Khama stands outside the entrance to the national legislature in Gaborone.

topple the pro-apartheid government in South Africa. Although Botswana denies this charge, South African planes have attacked across the border, killing Botswanans as well as South Africans.

Botswana experienced considerable stability under Seretse Khama. A small but vocal political opposition strengthened the discussion of important issues. In three elections—in 1969, 1974, and 1979—more

The coat of arms of the Republic of Botswana contains many symbolic elements. Two black-and-white zebras represent the mixed nature of the nation's population. One animal supports an elephant's ivory tusk, which symbolizes the country's wildlife, and the other zebra holds a head of sorghum—a major crop. Within the shield are three cog-wheels, which stand for manufacturing, and three wavy blue lines, which suggest Botswana's reliance on water. The cow's head is a reminder of the vital cattle industry. Beneath the entire illustration is the motto *pula,* which means "rain" or "let there be rain" in Setswana, the national language.

than one party campaigned for seats in the legislature. In each election, however, the BDP maintained its majority in the National Assembly.

Recent Events

In 1980 President Seretse Khama died of cancer, and his vice president and close associate, Quett Masire, succeeded him. Another multiparty election in September 1984 confirmed Masire as president, and the BDP again emerged as the dominant organization in the legislature.

President Masire's administration faces the challenge of restructuring relations with South Africa and of managing Botswana's economic growth. Zimbabwe's black-ruled government allows Botswana to send some goods through Zimbabwe to Beira—Mozambique's port on the Indian Ocean. The coming independence of Namibia may give Botswana another route to the sea. These two lanes of transportation could decrease Botswana's need to

In 1986 elementary-school students waved Botswana's flag during independence celebrations that commemorated 20 years of self-rule.

Seretse Khama's successor, Quett Masire, inspects a guard of honor during a national parade. A teacher, farmer, and journalist, Masire helped to found the Botswana Democratic party. He also is involved in several organizations that fight against apartheid.

To increase the family's total income, a significant number of Botswanan men work in South Africa's mining sector. Many of the miners remain in South Africa for long periods of time.

Among Botswana's new development programs are projects that tap solar energy. These solar panels operate a water pump that runs from a river to a village.

send most of its cargo through South Africa.

In addition, the Masire government is exploring new trade connections, particularly through the Southern African Development Coordination Conference (SADCC). Formed in 1980, the conference is made up of nine countries that rely economically on South Africa. The SADCC has provided a framework for regional cooperation to spur economic growth, to foster trade, and to achieve financial independence.

Although droughts have affected Botswana's livestock and harvests, the nation has enjoyed a strong economic position as a result of its diamond industry. In 1989 Botswana was the world's leading producer of gem-quality diamonds and got 80 percent of its export earnings from diamond sales. The government has funneled much of this money into strengthening rural development projects and into creating jobs. South African firms own shares in Botswana's mining industry, however, and the gems travel to overseas markets through South Africa. The issue of ties to South Africa, therefore, overshadows much of Botswana's future.

Government

Botswana is a parliamentary republic, with executive power vested in a president who is chosen by members of the one-house National Assembly. The chief executive's powers include calling and dissolving the assembly and approving all taxation bills. A cabinet drawn largely from the assembly assists the president.

The National Assembly consists of 34 directly elected members and 4 delegates that the president names. The legislature also has a non-voting attorney general and a speaker, both of whom are appointed. Citizens over the age of 21 can vote, and they choose assembly members by secret ballot.

The leaders of Botswana's eight principal Batswana groups continue to have secondary governmental functions. The traditional elite participate in district councils and serve on land boards. They play minor judicial roles and also continue to hold *kgotla* (public meetings). Before making some new laws, the legislature consults Batswana leaders regarding traditional Batswana concerns.

Botswana's Constitution of 1965 contains a code of human rights, which the nation's courts uphold. The judicial system consists of customary (traditional) and civil courts. Leaders of the various Batswana kingdoms preside over customary courts and exercise some power, most importantly in cases of cattle theft. Common law courts include magistrate courts and circuit courts of appeal. The High Court is located in Lobatse.

For administrative purposes, Botswana is divided into 10 district councils and 4 town councils. Each has an elected governing body and an executive commissioner. The councils finance primary education, supply licenses to local businesses, and collect taxes. They also help to plan development projects and to budget funds.

Courtesy of Department of Information and Broadcasting

A central part of Botswana's local government remains the *kgotla,* or public meeting, in which village elders make decisions through discussion and compromise with government officials.

Women perform a traditional Batswana dance during a competition in Mahalapye.

3) The People

About 1.2 million people inhabit Botswana's 231,000 square miles of territory. Another 50,000 Botswanans live outside the country, mostly in South Africa. Although the nation's average population density is low—five people per square mile—the population of Botswana is distributed very unevenly. The highest concentrations of people occur along a north-south corridor in the eastern portion of the country. In this area, the water supply is permanent, farmable land is available, and health care and schooling are adequate.

Because of a high birthrate and a low life expectancy, most of Botswana's population is very young. About half of all Botswanans are under the age of 15. The country contains significantly more females than males because many young men go to South Africa to work. Despite this migrant labor pattern, Botswana has a high population growth rate—3.4 percent—compared to many other African countries.

Ethnic and Language Groups

Botswana contains one large and a number of small ethnic groups. Many of these communities share cultural and language

Botswana has a high birthrate, and about 48 percent of the population is younger than 15 years of age.

traits. The Batswana—who have eight major subgroups—make up 95 percent of the African population in Botswana. They have a common history, language, and social organization. The Batswana are also closely related by language and culture to Basotho peoples who live in Lesotho (a small country surrounded by South Africa) and South Africa.

The Batswana have long dominated Botswana's other ethnic groups and continue to be influential in the government. Both of the country's presidents have come from the Batswana. Seretse Khama was a member of the Bangwato royal family, and Quett Masire is of the Bangwaketse subgroup.

The traditional pattern of Batswana society—in which an upper class rules the majority—continues in Botswana. Even Batswana subgroups are ranked in order of seniority, with the oldest—the Bakwena

Small villages—in which round, thatched dwellings are common—exist throughout eastern Botswana. More than three-fourths of Botswanans live in rural areas.

—usually at the top of the list. The Bangwato, which is the largest group in number, the Bangwaketse, and the Batawana generally follow the Bakwena in order. The remaining subgroups are the Bakgatla, the Balete, the Barolong, and the Batlokwa. Members of all of these clans speak Setswana—the Bantu language of the Batswana. Along with English, Setswana is the nation's official language.

The San, whose ancestors were the original inhabitants of the country, now number about 30,000. Of small physical stature, the San traditionally speak a click language, so called because the action of the tongue against the roof of the mouth produces a clicking sound. In Botswana, most San use the Nharo click language. Fewer than 5,000 San continue to live in traditional ways in the Kalahari Desert. Most members of the group work on farms or in cities, and many have adopted the Batswana culture that dominates the country.

Botswana's other minorities include the Bakalanga and the Bayei. Earlier in Bo-

The enlarged front and back of one pula—the national unit of money—shows both of the country's official languages, English and Setswana. President Masire appears on the front of the bill, and Botswana's coat of arms decorates the back.

A San hunter digs in the ground to find grubs (young, wormlike insects), which, when dried and ground up, he will use to poison the tips of arrows. Survival in harsh desert conditions is a key element in the traditional San lifestyle. The people live in small, mobile groups, always ready to leave an area in search of food and water. Few San continue to live in the age-old way, and many farm or work in towns.

tswana's history, the Batswana conquered these groups, transforming them into a labor force for Batswana needs. As a result, tension remains between these minorities—who make up about 1 percent of the population—and the dominant Batswana.

Customers mingle outside a cooperative supermarket in Gaborone. Although most Botswanans live in villages, the number of city dwellers is rising.

Sizable communities of black South Africans and Zimbabweans also live in the country. They have arrived in Botswana since the 1970s, when strife disrupted their homelands. Some Botswanans see these more recent immigrants as opportunists who seek citizenship so they can obtain high governmental and commercial positions.

Botswana is also home to many Europeans and white South Africans, some of whom raise livestock. Other whites—who benefit from a high-quality, Western education—occupy important technical and policy-making positions in national organizations and businesses. By providing proper training, the Masire administration seeks to bring more black Botswanans into the government.

Daily Life and Religion

Descendants of cattle herders and farmers, most modern-day Botswanans live at least partially off the land. But lack of rainfall and poor soil prevent the majority of Botswanans from producing enough food to feed their families.

41

More than 80 percent of Botswana's population reside in small villages or towns in the eastern third of the country. These settlements consist of a cluster of round, straw-roofed houses built of mud bricks. Some homes are constructed of cement blocks and have corrugated metal roofs.

Life in most Botswanan villages follows a traditional pattern. A male-dominated council, usually led by the head of the oldest or largest family, decides which part of the village land each family group will farm. Agricultural output remains low, and few people can support themselves solely by farming or keeping cattle. As a result, men leave their villages in search of temporary work, and Botswanan women carry the double burden of farming and raising a family. Women often hand over the daily care of their babies to grandparents or very young girls.

With their long history of organized settlement, most Batswana continue to support some traditional African beliefs. These ideas often revolve around the powers and responsibilities of local rulers and healers.

Among daily chores for Botswanan women is pounding grain into flour, which is then made into porridge.

Most dwellings in Botswana have roofs of straw. Here, a worker applies a new covering to a round, pointed frame.

On a cold morning, a village leader *(left)* enjoys a meal with his wife and grandchildren. In rural areas, a shaded space in the family compound is set aside for cooking and eating.

Leaders of Faith Gospel After Christ, a small Christian sect that mixes African and Christian traditions, meet to discuss the wedding of two young Botswanans.

Spiritual meaning is attached to nature, to the presence of rain, and to good health. Believers regard individual actions as the causes of sickness and drought. They also have deep respect for their dead relatives.

Because of missionary activity in the nineteenth century, about 15 percent of the population are practicing Christians. A much larger number mixes Christian and traditional beliefs. Most Christians follow Protestant faiths.

The San have their own set of religious ideas, which honor nature and respect a divine creator. Dance rituals are important to traditional San believers, and men sometimes go into a trance while dancing. The San consider this state a form of communication between humans and a supernatural power.

The Arts

Dance, music, storytelling, weaving, and crafts are enduring traditions in Botswa-

Before his performance begins, a guitarist tunes his instrument. Along with traditional types of music, Botswanans enjoy popular forms, some of which originate outside the country.

A display of handwoven baskets shows the variety of styles and designs that weavers can achieve.

na. These arts make up an important part of daily life. Local art councils and museums—as well as the Botswana Society—also help to ensure the growth of these elements of national culture.

Founded in 1968, the Botswana Society encourages literary work in the social sciences, arts, and humanities. It publishes *Botswana Notes and Records,* which contains articles of interest on various aspects of life in Botswana. Another source of cultural unity is Radio Botswana, which broadcasts news and educational programs in both English and Setswana.

The writings of the late author Leetile Disang Raditladi and of Michael Seboni preserve the Batswana heritage. The works of both men appear in Setswana. A politician as well as an author, Raditladi wrote award-winning plays and poetry. Seboni began his literary career in the 1960s with a children's novel entitled *Rammone of the Kalahari.* He also writes traditional poems

Like basketry, Botswanan pottery comes in many shapes and sizes. These examples have been hand painted with traditional patterns of flowers and dots.

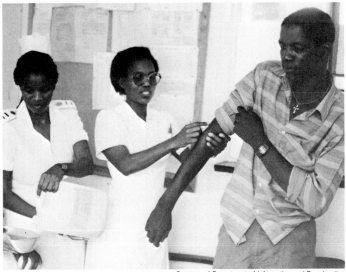

At a rural clinic, a patient calmly undergoes immunization. Although the younger population is still afflicted by childhood diseases, a national vaccination program has decreased the frequency of some common illnesses.

and has translated Shakespeare's plays *The Merchant of Venice* and *Henry IV* into Setswana.

Since independence, many people have revived age-old arts and have introduced some new techniques. Handwoven rugs and wall hangings from Odi (near Gaborone) and Serowe are recent additions to a growing export industry. Leatherworking and basket weaving—long-established crafts throughout southern Africa—now are part of an expanding market.

Health

Before independence, the colonial government spent little money on developing medical facilities. Missionaries staffed and funded most health clinics. Since 1966, however, Botswana has set aside significant portions of its budget to improve the health of its citizens.

National campaigns to vaccinate babies against major diseases—such as tuberculosis, polio, measles, and whooping cough —have reached about 90 percent of the

45

one-year-olds in Botswana. Yet poor sanitation, substandard diets, and hard-to-reach medical services continue to endanger the health of children and adults.

In 1990 the infant mortality rate was 72 deaths in every 1,000 live births—a relatively low figure compared to the rest of Africa. Yet many babies die before they are two years old because of poor nutrition. Only one doctor exists for every 10,000 people, and few Botswanan homes have adequate sanitary facilities. As a result of these conditions, the average life expectancy at birth is 57 years.

Education

Education is available very unevenly throughout Botswana. Money spent on education in the 1970s increased the number of primary schools in the countryside, but less than 50 percent of the teachers in rural schools are qualified. Almost 90 percent of urban elementary teachers have good educational training, and they teach smaller classes.

About 80 percent of Botswana's young people attend elementary school. Only 15 percent, however, go on to secondary classes. Wealthy people send their children to private schools, where lessons are taught in English. In general, courses in Botswanan schools—which focus on practical learning—are taught in Setswana. In the late 1980s, the country's overall literacy rate—in either Setswana or English—was about 62 percent.

Until the 1970s, only four government-run secondary schools existed in Botswana. Christian mission societies operated six other secondary schools, and the University of Botswana, Lesotho, and Swaziland (UBLS) provided higher education. Located in Roma, Lesotho, UBLS became

Two young pupils work side by side in a rural classroom. Facilities and teacher training are better in urban areas than they are in the countryside.

the property of the Lesotho government in 1975. Botswana opened its own post-secondary school in Gaborone in 1982. The University of Botswana offers undergraduate certificates in several fields, including educational and medical training.

Sports and Recreation

Sports are an important part of the country's social life, and soccer—called football in Botswana—is the most popular team activity and spectator sport. Competition within a national league and matches between villages generate considerable interest. Intense rivalries, which sometimes reflect political differences, exist between teams.

For the majority of Botswanans, conversation and storytelling are the main forms of recreation. Dance halls, bars, and movie theaters exist in most towns and are very

Photo by Michael Kahn/The Hutchison Library

Graduates from the University of Botswana listen attentively to graduation speeches. Students at the school can receive training in education, medicine, or science. The university's total enrollment in the late 1980s was under 2,000.

Courtesy of John C. Mason

A high-jump competition at a secondary school draws a large crowd of spectators. About 15 percent of Botswanans of high-school age attend classes.

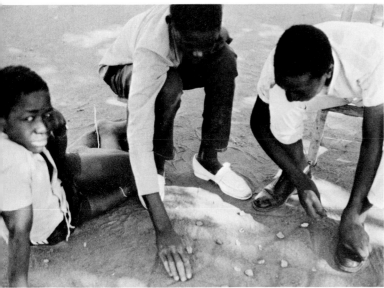

Courtesy of John C. Mason

popular meeting places for people at all levels of society.

In urban areas, athletic clubs have been established, mainly for the wealthy. Gambling casinos are a new feature of city life, usually attracting tourists from South Africa. An 18-hole golf course is centrally located in the capital, and swimming pools exist in major towns. A small yacht club is situated at the Gaborone Dam, where sailing and windsurfing are favorite activities. Horseback riding is also popular.

Food

The relatively fertile lands in the east and in the inland delta of the Okavango provide most of Botswana's food. Three crops —millet, corn, and cassava—form the basis of the national diet.

Farmers have cultivated millet and corn in Botswana for centuries. A tall, strong plant with a large head of grain, millet grows five to six feet high. After being harvested, millet is pounded into flour with a large wooden pole and is made into a porridge called *bogobe*. Botswanans also grow corn, which is occasionally grilled on the cob. Most corn, however, is mashed

into another form of porridge—the staple of the Botswanan diet.

Resembling a hard potato, cassavas are large, long roots. Botswanans eat raw cassavas in the fields, bake them in the embers

Courtesy of Department of Information and Broadcasting

This woman is sifting grains to remove the unwanted husks. After this step is complete, the kernels will be pounded into flour.

48

of small fires, or soak and grate them into a coarse flour. Cassava flour has little nutritional value, although it can be stored for weeks and is relatively easy to transport. Cooks often add spices and seeds to the flour to season it.

Most Botswanans regularly eat a combination of millet, cassava, and corn, plus a little sugar, tea, and processed food. *Bojalwa*, a locally brewed beer made from cereal grains, is also popular. Except on ceremonial occasions, meat is rarely available to the ordinary Botswanan.

Wealthier members of society, in contrast, often eat chicken, eggs, beef, fruit, and vegetables. A typical meal for the rich might consist of pumpkin or squash soup, followed by chicken or charcoal-grilled beef with potatoes. A salad of locally grown lettuce, tomatoes, onions, and green beans might complete the main meal. Dessert could include fresh melon, mangoes, or papayas (large yellow fruits). The diners often drink beer with the meal. A growing number of urban people eat imported foods prepared in a European style.

In some areas, cooks bake loaves of bread in traditional mud ovens.

A thick, foaming head is a characteristic of Botswanan beer, which is often made in an earthenware pot.

Two young children fetch water from a local well. Because only about half of the nation's rural families have access to safe water, some groups have a very poor standard of living. This fact contrasts with the average national income, which is high compared to most African countries.

4) The Economy

Botswana is an economic puzzle. On the one hand, the country contains many minerals, such as diamonds, copper, nickel, and coal. These deposits offer diversity in a primarily agricultural economy. On the other hand, most Botswanans are poor. Although the average yearly income per person is about $1,000—a high amount in Africa—over half of the rural people and two-thirds of the urban dwellers live in poverty. Yet, a small section of the soci-ety—drawn from the traditional Batswana ruling class—is quite wealthy because income is distributed unevenly.

Most Botswanans have to hold more than one job to earn a living. For example, although more than 85 percent of the rural population try to grow crops, this activity accounts for less than 35 percent of their income. Rural Botswanans depend on the wages of family members who work full-time in the cities or in the mines of

Courtesy of Department of Information and Broadcasting

Many rural people supplement their earnings by taking jobs as miners. These workers at the Selebi-Phikwe complex extract copper and nickel from underground pits.

High-quality cattle await slaughtering in Lobatse. A small percentage of Botswana's population owns most of the livestock.

Photo by Michael Kahn/The Hutchison Library

Botswana and South Africa. These migrant laborers, who continue to maintain ties with their rural households, often own cattle and get their food from home.

Because of these conditions, the quality of life for most Botswanans is uncertain. People are constantly on the move—to and from jobs in Botswana and South Africa, to and from one patch of farmland to another, and in search of grass and water for livestock.

Although foreign trade is an important aspect of the nation's economy, Botswana lacks its own seaport. Few good roads exist, and South Africa runs the railway that crosses that nation from Botswana to the sea. As a result, sending goods to overseas markets is still difficult. In addition, different standards of living reflect an unequal distribution of wealth. Rich landowners control huge tracts of grazing land, a situation that hampers plans for increasing the number of livestock. High unemployment and underemployment, dependence on foreign aid, and the continued dominance of the Batswana upper class have interfered with Botswana's economic growth.

Mining

Since the 1970s, mining has transformed Botswana's economy. The rapid expansion of local mining activities has generated jobs and considerable foreign income. Diamonds account for about 80 percent of the country's total export earnings, and Botswana has become the largest diamond producer in the world.

South Africa's De Beers Company and the Botswana government jointly own the nation's diamond mines. The pits at Orapa, Jwaneng, and Letlhakane contain substantial deposits. These finds should yield diamonds for at least 30 more years.

Courtesy of Eleanore Woollard

An aerial view of the diamond mine at Jwaneng shows the area excavated for diamond ore. Once the gems have been extracted, they go to the capital for sorting by quality.

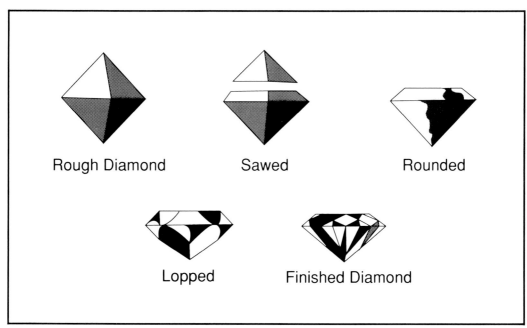

Rough Diamond   Sawed   Rounded

Lopped   Finished Diamond

Diamonds are the hardest substance in the world. The wrong cut of a diamond can change it from an expensive gem to a stone of lesser quality. Although Botswana has a small diamond-cutting industry, many stones are sent abroad for finishing.

About 13 million carats (the unit of weight for precious stones) of gem-quality diamonds are produced each year. Botswana's diamond industry directly employs almost 8,000 people, and many more jobs result from the need for support services.

The Selebi-Phikwe nickel and copper mines employ about 5,000 people and account for about 10 percent of the country's export earnings. Although Botswana annually produced about 50,000 tons of copper and nickel in the 1980s, low world prices caused the mines to lose money.

Over 17 million tons of coal are thought to exist in eastern Botswana. Coal mining began in 1972, and since then miners have extracted as much as 400,000 tons a year. Shell Oil and the national government have reached an agreement to develop the Kgaswe coalfield near Palapye when the global market price for coal increases. Shipping coal from large reserves at Serowe and Mmamabula will be easier when construction is completed on a railway between the

The site at Selebi-Phikwe contains not only a complex to mine copper and nickel but also a power station to generate electricity.

53

A conveyor belt carries chunks of coal away from the mine at Morupule.

Kalahari Desert and the South Atlantic coast.

Although jobs and revenue have resulted from mining, the industry has also caused some problems. The number of people who leave their villages to search for work in the mines is greater than the available jobs. Unemployed mine workers remain in or near mining towns, establishing makeshift housing. Selebi-Phikwe, for example, has a large squatter settlement. In addition, some of the polluted waste from mine operations flows into the nation's rivers, which endangers Botswana's limited water supply.

Agriculture

Although mining earns greater income, herding and farming employ more Botswanans. About 85 percent of the people raise livestock or farm the land. Because the country's soil is more suited to producing pasture than crops, livestock dominate the

When rain levels are normal, pans in the Kalahari Desert fill up and allow grasses suitable for grazing to grow. The country contains more cattle than people.

agricultural sector. Indeed, cattle outnumber humans by three to one. Botswana's second major export earner, the cattle industry produces about 10 percent of the nation's foreign income. Although the number of cattle tripled in the decade after independence, droughts and overgrazing have since reduced herds considerably.

Botswana is one of the main livestock producers in southern Africa, and beef is a major export. Historically, only members of royal or very wealthy Batswana families could own cattle. This long-established tradition has concentrated one-half of the total cattle in the hands of 5 percent of the people. The rest of the nation's livestock feed on the grazing lands of low-income herders, where modern breeding methods and efficient veterinary care are uncommon. Owning few animals, small-scale herders are reluctant to part with their cattle or to upgrade their stock. To earn money, the farmers bring their cattle to slaughterhouses in Lobatse and Maun.

Courtesy of Eleanore Woollard

At harvesttime, a farmer uses a homemade alarm system to scare birds away from his crop.

Photo by Michael Kahn/The Hutchison Library

Workers pack a portion of the nation's tomato crop, which farmers plant mostly in northeastern Botswana.

Goats and sheep roam freely in most of Botswana. Since the 1960s, drought and disease have reduced the total number of these animals to less than one million. Farmers raise other livestock—such as chickens, turkeys, and ducks—throughout the country. Some companies have tried large-scale poultry production near Gaborone and other urban areas. Botswana produces enough eggs to meet the demands of the small number of people who can afford to buy them.

In general, the nation's soil is not very fertile. Only 5 percent of Botswana receives enough rainfall to make farming easy. Even in these areas, however, precipitation levels vary, and water evaporates quickly. Thus, plants lose water so rapidly that crops sometimes fail even in years of normal rainfall. Since 1982 the country has faced a persistent drought. Despite the availability of underground water supplies, lack of rain has cut the production of crops and livestock, particularly by small-scale farmers.

The major food crops—cowpeas, corn, millet, sorghum, and several varieties of vegetables—are not produced in sufficient quantities for the country's own needs. Botswana's total grain crop is less than 15,000 tons, and the nation's demand exceeds 200,000 tons annually. As a result,

A Botswanan herder gets a bucket of milk from his cow.

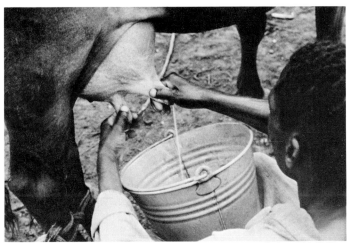

Courtesy of John C. Mason

Courtesy of Department of Information and Broadcasting

Modern sprinkling methods are an effective way to water cropland. Not many farmers, however, can afford this up-to-date technology.

Botswana imports increasing amounts of food, mostly from South Africa.

Through development programs and marketing boards, government planners have tried to broaden Botswana's agricultural output. Farmers are planting more cash-earning crops, such as peanuts, cotton, and sunflowers, in fields near the Tuli Block in eastern Botswana. With the advice of the People's Republic of China, a small rice-growing project was started in the Okavango Delta. Citrus fruits, which farmers cultivated before independence, continue to grow well in eastern Botswana.

A field of sorghum, one of the country's main grain crops, ripens in the summer sun.

Manufacturing

Although manufacturing has expanded considerably since 1980, it occupies a distant third place in the national economy. A small domestic market and the availability of South African goods hamper the growth of Botswana's industrial sector. Roughly 85 percent of Botswana's manufactured goods come from South Africa. A critical shortage of skilled laborers also hinders industrialization in Botswana.

Meat processing is the most valuable manufacturing activity, and the Botswana Meat Commission (BMC) dominates this sector. The BMC's facilities in Lobatse—among the largest processing plants in Africa—can slaughter about 1,000 head of cattle daily. A smaller slaughterhouse is located at Maun. Meat canning and preparing livestock by-products, such as hides and skins, are other activities of the cattle industry.

Other manufacturing plants in Botswana tend to be small, and foreigners own most of them. Few businesses exist in rural areas, and the factories that operate in the larger towns together employ less than 10,000 people. Some of these firms weave cloth, make clothing, and assemble furniture. Since the 1970s, a small diamond-cutting industry has developed. Most of Botswana's diamonds are exported and become valuable gems.

Workers at the Lobatse plant of the Botswana Meat Commission skin the carcasses of freshly slaughtered cattle. The facility, one of the largest in Africa, provides meat to European and African countries. Small-scale herders do not often slaughter their livestock. Instead, they trade their animals for crops that they cannot grow themselves.

57

Among Botswana's developing industries are small cooperative ventures, where people share the work and profits of their enterprise. These women are silk-screening fabric with designs of butterflies.

A fair amount of manufacturing involves final-stage assembly or the repacking of imports for retail sales. In 1988 Botswana and Zimbabwe disagreed about goods being exported from Botswana. Zimbabwe charged that the items had originated in South Africa, with whom Zimbabwe officially refuses to trade. Although Botswana and Zimbabwe agreed not to become involved in a trade dispute, they did not resolve the question of Botswana selling products whose parts originate in South Africa.

Trade

Botswana belongs to the Southern African Customs Union (SACU), which the British created in 1910. The SACU links the economies of Botswana, Lesotho, South Africa, and Swaziland. South Africa determines and collects the taxes on goods exchanged among the four countries. The South African government then pays each nation a share of the collections. This revenue accounted for about 15 percent of Botswana's annual budget in the 1980s. Anti-apartheid governments in the region are pressuring Botswana to withdraw from the SACU and to make a trade agreement with other anti-apartheid states, such as Zimbabwe.

In 1976 Botswana introduced the pula —a national currency to replace the South African rand that the nation had been using. The country's leaders also explored other trade connections in southern Africa, notably the Southern African Development Coordination Conference (SADCC). With its main office in Gaborone, the SADCC may broaden Botswana's commercial contacts.

The government has sought ties with African nations to the north, with Arab countries, and with states that are part of the European Community (EC). Nevertheless, Botswana's main trading partners remain South Africa, Great Britain, Zimbabwe, and the United States.

Foreign Aid and Tourism

Throughout the 1980s, the nation's balance of earnings and debt repayments has been about even. Indeed, Botswana had about $2 billion in foreign currency reserves in 1989. This healthy economic situation results from diamond exports, from money sent home by Botswanan workers in South Africa, and from substantial foreign aid. The United States, Canada, West Germany, Norway, Sweden, the World Health Organization, the EC, and the World Bank have loaned or given Botswana money. These funds make up about 40 percent of the total budget for development in Botswana, forming a foreign debt that is equal to about one-third of the nation's annual income.

Tourism is another economic activity that brings foreign money into Botswana. In the 1980s, facilities were upgraded near all national parks—the main focus of tourist journeys. Located in Gaborone, the Department of Wildlife, National Parks, and Tourism runs a network of protected game sanctuaries. Some shops in large towns sell goods made from the skins of Botswana's wild animals. Largely meant to attract tourists, these items deplete the nation's wildlife population and cause concern about the government's animal protection policies.

Seasonal rains draw wildlife to the Chobe River between April and November. As a result, these months are the busiest season for Chobe National Park. A series of roads takes vacationers through areas where giraffes, elephants, and rare white rhinoceroses can be viewed. The Moremi Wildlife Reserve, located on the edge of the Okavango Delta, is also very popular. Rougher

Photo by Michael Kahn/The Hutchison Library

President Masire opens a summit meeting of the Southern African Development Coordination Conference (SADCC). Established in 1980, the SADCC has nine member-countries, each of which addresses an issue of mutual concern. Botswana focuses on controlling animal diseases and shares its knowledge with fellow conference members.

A sign *(left)* welcomes visitors to Chobe National Park, where giraffes *(above)* and ostriches *(below)* are among the animals that are able to live in relative safety from hunters and poachers.

than Chobe, this park has only dirt tracks running through it. Visitors usually need four-wheel-drive vehicles to see the region's large herds of zebras, wildebeests, kudu, and eland (antelope). Dozens of bird species also frequent the reserve.

Transportation and Energy

Botswana lacks a well-developed transportation system. The main railway line from South Africa to Zimbabwe passes through the eastern part of Botswana. National Railways of Zimbabwe owned and operated this railroad until 1984. In that year, the section from Ramatlabama to Mahalapye was given to Botswana, which took control of the track within the country. Branch lines serve the Selebi-Phikwe mining complex and the coal mines at Morupule.

Zimbabwe's independence in 1980 opened up to Botswana an alternative trade route through Zimbabwe to the Indian Ocean port of Beira, Mozambique. As a result, Botswana's transport and communications were no longer as dependent upon the South African network. Nevertheless, guerrilla warfare in Mozambique hampers the use of the Beira facilities.

Botswana has about 2,000 miles of paved roads. About 7,000 miles of earth-and-sand routes also cross the country. The highway from Gaborone to Kazungula—where the borders of Botswana, Namibia, Zambia, and Zimbabwe meet—is tarred, as is the Palapye-to-Serowe road. Few Botswanans own cars, and most people travel by foot, bicycle, or animal-drawn vehicle.

The center of Botswana's air network is Seretse Khama Airport, which opened in 1984. From this international landing field in Gaborone, Air Botswana, Royal Swazi National Airways, and Zambia Airways operate regular services to South Africa, Zambia, and Zimbabwe. Regional airports and smaller airfields are located at all

At Letlhakane, where a diamond mine is located, a resident carries water back to her home.

A tractor-drawn bush helps to smooth the potholes of a dirt-and-sand pathway. In most areas, local roads are unpaved.

Photo by The Hutchison Library

Completed in 1986, the Gaborone Dam overflowed when heavy rains finally came in 1988, after seven years of drought.

Courtesy of Eleanore Woollard

major population centers and tourist sites. An active charter service carries 40 percent of the passengers that fly into Botswanan airports.

Except for coal and recently discovered deposits of natural gas, Botswana lacks its own fuel sources. The nation imports most of its petroleum and electricity from South Africa. The Shashe Dam and power station, located in northeastern Botswana along the Shashe River, provide the Selebi-Phikwe area with water and electrical energy. Government planners are investi-

gating the possibility of harnessing the flow of other rivers in the country.

The Future

Internal conditions, as well as international politics, affect Botswana's prospects. Traditional landowning patterns and social structures favor members of the Batswana upper class. These age-old ways hold back economic output. A growing number of the nation's citizens lack jobs and have a low standard of living.

Botswana's major problem remains its relations with South Africa. Development projects, such as the proposed railway through Namibia, were long jeopardized by South Africa's military occupation of Namibia. Apartheid policies, which Botswana publicly rejects, continue to affect Botswana's stability. Apartheid's rules affect Botswanans who work in South African mines. Some black South Africans seek refuge in Botswana from the restrictions of apartheid.

Despite these concerns, the nation's future looks promising. Mineral-rich, Botswana has considerable mining potential, particularly in the north and east. In addition, the SADCC intends to coordinate transportation and communication links among its nine southern African member-countries. This plan may further improve Botswana's internal network of roads and railways, as well as reduce its dependence on South Africa.

Botswana's strengths include a stable political situation. Skilled in the complex politics of southern Africa, the country's leaders seem ready to meet the challenges of social change and economic growth that the nation may face in the twenty-first century.

A young, enthusiastic Botswanan celebrates the country's independence day by waving the national flag.

Courtesy of John C. Mason

Index